The Accidental Adventures of INDIA McALLISTER

The Accidental Adventures of

INDIA McALLISTER

written and illustrated by

Charlotte Agell

Christy Ottaviano Books

Henry Holt and Company ☆ New York

Thanks to Ragan Bartlett, Kelly Conley, Merry Kahn, Karyn Smith, Chia-Ju Hsieh, Henry Hodder, and Julia Beatty (whose short story was so full of wisdom), and to *all* the students and staff at HMS and YES in Yarmouth, Maine. Thanks also to Sarah and Gemma Laurence for much encouragement, as well as to Matthea Daughtry and her family (including the inspiring Bird!), and to my Haystack group. Much gratitude to Christy Ottaviano, editor extraordinaire, as well as to Edite Kroll, wonderful agent. As always, to my family (Denison! McDonald! Agell! Simmons!)—especially Peter, Anna, and Jon.

Henry Holt and Company, LLC, *Publishers since 1866*
175 Fifth Avenue, New York, New York 10010
www.HenryHoltKids.com

Henry Holt® is a registered trademark of Henry Holt and Company, LLC.

Distributed in Canada by H. B. Fenn and Company Ltd.

Library of Congress Cataloging-in-Publication Data
Agell, Charlotte.
The accidental adventures of India McAllister / Charlotte Agell. — 1st ed.
p. cm.
"Christy Ottaviano Books."
Summary: India, an unusual nine-and-a-half-year-old living in small-town Maine, has a series of adventures which bring her closer to her artist-mother, strengthen her friendship with a neighbor boy, and help her to accept the man for whom her father moved away.
ISBN 978-0-8050-8902-8
[1. Friendship—Fiction. 2. Family life—Maine—Fiction. 3. Divorce—Fiction. 4. Homosexuality—Fiction. 5. Chinese Americans—Fiction. 6. Maine—Fiction.] I. Title.
PZ7.A2665Acc 2010 [Fic]—dc22 2009018907

First edition—2010 / Designed by Véronique Lefèvre Sweet
Printed in May 2010 in the United States of America by
R. R. Donnelley & Sons Company, Harrisonburg, Virginia

1 3 5 7 9 10 8 6 4 2

To Frank, who puts the dad in stepfather,
and to Mia, grade four!

Contents

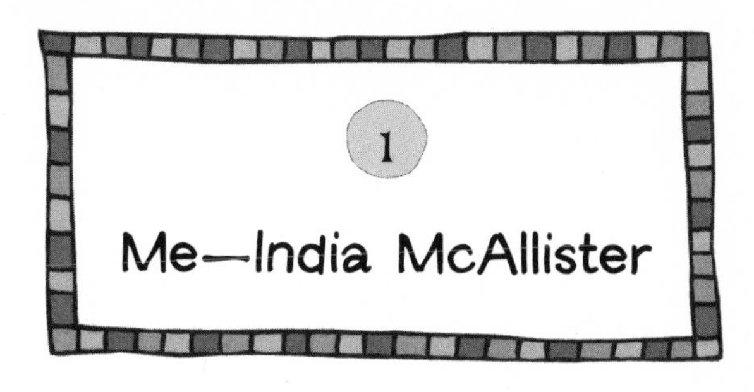

1 Me—India McAllister

My name is India McAllister, and I'm nine and a half years old. I live in Wolfgang, Maine, where there are no wolves, but the coyotes grow almost as big. You can hear them calling to each other at night.

My house is on the corner of Blueberry and Buckle streets, so my address sounds like the best breakfast in the world: blueberry buckle! Nowadays, it's just Mom and me, and Tofu of course. He's my dog. It's a big house with really high ceilings. You could practically play basketball in here. I've never done that, but badminton works okay, except when the birdie gets stuck in the chandelier.

We actually have a chandelier, but we never dust it, and I can't seem to knock down that birdie.

Everybody always asks me about my name. People think I'm from India. But I'm not. My mom and dad adopted me from China, back when I was too little to remember. The way I look at it, I'm from Wolfgang, Maine. Here's what I'm *not* named for:

Except for being born in China, I've never even been outside of Maine. Here's what I *am* named for: → 

That's because Rosemary, my mother, is an artist, and she's in love with ink. *India* ink. She says it's the best smell on earth and that it's darker than night. I think it's okay, but personally I prefer sour apple gum, or how the grass smells when it gets cut.

Right now, Mom isn't working much in ink. She's in an oil paint phase. Since her studio is in the big front room, our house smells like turpentine. That room used to be the parlor, Mom says, back when fancy people lived in this house, instead of us.

Once upon a time, my dad lived at the corner of Blueberry and Buckle, too. His name is Andrew. He isn't fancy either, but at least he lived here. Now he lives in Ottenbury with his friend Richard. He left when I was seven, but sometimes it doesn't feel that long ago. I see him all the time—almost every weekend. But I miss him more than that.

I don't miss Richard. I don't really *know* Richard.

My mother says she doesn't care. Divorce is fine with her. Mom insists she's so busy painting these days that she can hardly think of anything else (except me, of course). And she is busy—very busy. She even forgets when to cook. It's a good thing I can put together a balanced meal by myself.

Our whole back room is full of paintings. Sometimes she sells one in a big show in New York City and is excited for weeks. Mom promises that next time she has a show there, we'll both go. Too bad for Dad. He'll be stuck in Ottenbury with Richard.

There's a lot to know about me. Like what I like. What people like is very revealing. For example, Richard likes smelly cheese.

I do not!

Here's what I do like . . .

India McAllister's Top Ten List!

1. Tofu. He's the best dog in the world, even if he eats our slippers.

2. Some of my mom's paintings. Not all of them. And my mom, of course.
3. My teacher, Mr. Argentoth. He lets me read when he's teaching. Also, he has the mustache of a grand villain, only he's really, really nice!

4. Colby, my best friend. He's a boy, but half the time, I act more like a boy than he does. (In third grade, that didn't matter. Amanda Roden says it matters now because we're in fourth grade, but I say it doesn't. Amanda Roden is *not* on the top ten list of what I like, or even my top hundred list, and there are definitely good reasons for that!!!!!)
5. My dad when we do cool stuff together. Actually, my dad *all* the time, except when he calls me on the phone. For some reason, I hate phones. Everything I say on the phone sounds like someone else talking.
6. Science. It just makes more sense than most things.

7. The crab apple tree in the middle of town. It's great for climbing. When the blossoms are out in May, nobody can see you, which is why I spent a whole day up there, but that's too long a story for a list.
8. Reading. I'm suspicious of people who don't like to read, although Colby is one of them, and I like him fine. He's just wrong about reading.

9. My next-door neighbor, Mrs. Ordinance. Her last name means "rule" but she hardly has any—rules, that is. When I want to hear myself think, I go to her house, and she listens.
10. Adventures. I haven't really had any yet, but I am planning to.

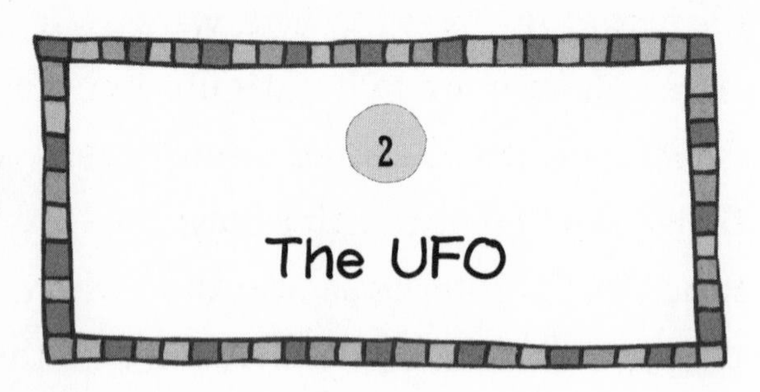

2
The UFO

One rainy Saturday I'm lying on top of my covers, listening to the rain, with no clue at all that I'm about to find adventure. I'm already dressed, but this day does not inspire me. It was *supposed* to be Dad Day, but he and Richard are in Venice, as in Italy.

There aren't many streets in Venice, just canals. The only thing is, the water is rising and kind of polluted. They figured they'd go see Venice before it disappears into the sea.

Mr. Argentoth, my teacher, says that a lot of stuff is going to disappear into the sea if we're not better at taking care of our planet. This makes me mad. Who is going to save the polar bear?

Wolfgang is pretty far from the ocean, so I am not too worried about rising water. It takes at least two hours to get to the shore, even if you speed, like Mom does. (She only gets speeding tickets when I'm not in the car, reminding her to slow down, for heaven's sake, or at least mine!)

So anyhow, Mom is painting, as usual, and there doesn't seem to be a particular reason to get out of bed, but then Colby shows up.

"India!"

He always walks right in and hollers my name.

I get out of bed and slide down the banister. Then we both walk up the stairs and slide down the banister three times each. It's a good thing to do at my house, on account of our elegant stairs.

After we get tired of that, Colby asks me if I want to see something wicked cool.

Who can resist?

But he won't tell me what it is.

"Then it wouldn't be a surprise," he says.

So I get my rain boots and my jacket, but no umbrella because those just get in the way unless you feel like parachuting off a fence or something.

That doesn't work too well, actually, but maybe with a stronger umbrella . . .

We walk down Buckle Street, me and Colby, and Tofu, who is finding every possible puddle.

We pass the old Greek church, which is boarded up and haunted. That's okay. Ghosts don't scare Colby or me in the daytime. We walk by the little brook, which is full of water and whooshing toward the lake, since it's spring. We walk past Amanda Roden's house, which I refuse to even look at.

"Wonder what the Rodent's up to?" Colby asks, but even though he calls her that sometimes, he doesn't think she's that bad.

I do.

Anyhow, we don't see her.

"Where are you taking me?" I finally ask.

She thinks she's so smart.

"Here," says Colby, stopping by a big field where there's nothing growing yet since it's only the end of April.

"What?" I ask, looking around. "Mud clumps?"

"No, silly," he says, pointing. "Don't you see?"

I look more closely.

"Come on," he says, and we start walking

across the field. It's a good thing we're both wearing boots, that's all I can say!

We reach a funny track in the mud. It wanders all over the place.

"So," he says. "*Now* can you see it?"

"What?" I still don't get it. So what if somebody drove all over the field? The farmer might not be happy, but it's hardly big news.

"A UFO," whispers Colby, and even Tofu stops bouncing around. "What else would make this weird pattern on a field?"

Sam Cook on his dirt bike, I want to say, but I don't since he has a point. If you stand back and look, you can tell: These are no ordinary tracks.

"These tracks are fresh," says Colby, squinting at the evidence. "The aliens must have been here in the night."

Tofu paws at the ground and whines.

"It's okay, boy," I say, sort of under my breath.

We decide to come back tonight and watch for UFOs even though it's probably strange to think that they'd visit the same place twice.

"Or not strange," says Colby, who's been watching some show about flying saucers. "They are drawn to places of power."

There's a place of power in Wolfgang? And it's Farmer Bixby's field? It doesn't seem that likely to me, but on the other hand, those tracks kind of made the hair on the back of my neck stand up. Something odd is going on.

So we do something highly unusual and lie to our moms. I tell mine that I'm going to sleep over at Colby's. He tells his he's going to sleep over at my house. I don't know why we don't tell them we're going to sleep out in the field. It just seems like the UFO might not come back if we broadcast the information all over Wolfgang.

Maybe they can read our brain waves.

It feels really weird, lying to my mom. She trusts me. Colby has two brothers and three sisters, so it's busy enough over at his house that he might not be missed even if he didn't say a word. But at our house, it's only the two of us and Tofu, so everything I do is extra obvious.

We bring our sleeping bags. My dad gave me mine for the camping trips that we hardly ever take since Richard. It's red with a really soft blue flannel lining, and it's so warm that I could probably use it at the South Pole. I love it a lot.

Colby's sleeping bag smells like mothballs and has two rips covered in duct tape, but I don't say anything. He can't help it if everything he owns is a hand-me-down.

Fortunately, by the time we get going, the rain has stopped. There's even a long, lovely sunset, with gold and red in the sky—the kind that always makes me think of angels.

We walk back to the field, talking and joking, but already I miss Tofu. It would have been nice to have him with us. (I try not to think about bears or coyotes.) But Mom would have suspected something if I said Tofu was going on a sleepover, too, so he had to stay home.

We spread out the sleeping bags on the little grassy hill next to the muddy field.

"Should've brought a tarp," says Colby, and he's right. The ground is damp. Colby digs a giant bag of BBQ chips out of his backpack, the kind we both hate but can't help eating because they're delicious in a too-salty way. Pretty soon, we've gobbled up half the bag and we're dying for something to drink. But we don't have anything. I experiment with sucking some of the rain off the grass. That helps for a second or two.

Maybe being unprepared is what makes it an adventure?

The sun drops into the trees at the edge of the field and hangs there for a while. I keep thinking how cool it is that our sun is really a star, burning in space. If we weren't so close to it, we'd see all the other stars in daytime (and be really, really cold). By the time our day star has set and the night stars come out, it is absolutely, tooth-chatteringly freezing.

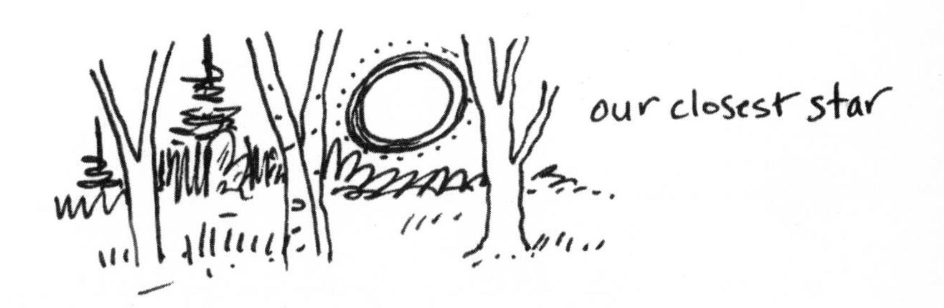

We crawl into our sleeping bags wearing all our clothes and talk about stuff. For example, whether Amanda Roden is in love with Tim Nickle, and if dogs can see in color. It's always easier to talk in the dark, when you don't have to look a person in the eye. We try to ignore the fact that the wind whooshing in the trees sounds like faraway screaming, and that we're lying there waiting for space aliens.

So far, there's nothing going on in the sky (except a bizarre cloud), which is a big relief to me since I'm starting to get a bit worried about actually seeing something. I mean, what would we do if a shining disk landed on the field and green men walked out of it? Not that I see why space aliens have to be green men. . . . Personally, I think it's a whole lot more likely that they look like something we can't even imagine. And that we're completely not what they thought we'd be, either. Especially the Rodent. Who would have ever thought *her* up?

And why is she so popular?

But we don't see a thing, maybe because we have our eyes shut tight. I'm just about asleep (despite the screaming wind) when Colby asks me if I know the facts of life.

"Of course I do," I mumble, thinking he means *What's the world's longest river?* (either the Nile or the Amazon, depending on how you measure it) and that sort of thing. I'm one of the smartest kids in our grade, even if I don't go around bragging about it.

But it turns out he doesn't mean that at all!

The facts of life are about how babies get made, and I absolutely cannot believe a word he is saying.

"Shut up," I tell him, even though he stopped talking minutes ago. I don't want to think about his crazy ideas anymore, at least not now. And, suddenly, I don't have to, because there's a strange flash in the sky. It's kind of greenish and quick. Colby gasps, and I grab his shoulder, but then after that there is nothing else. The sky stays dark and starry, and the wind even dies down, but we sit there in our wet sleeping bags, hardly daring to breathe.

"I think that *was* one," I whisper when my mouth finally works again.

"Maybe," Colby whispers back.

"So now we can leave, right?"

"Fine with me," he says, worming out of his bag.

We run all the way through the dark woods and the quiet streets back to my house, which is where we have most of our sleepovers since we have so much extra room.

It's a good thing that people don't lock their doors around here. According to our kitchen clock it's 2:15 in the morning. Tofu bounces down the stairs and jumps all over us, but Mom stays asleep. Colby and I roll out our damp sleeping bags on the living room floor, with Tofu snuggled in between us. He snorts in his sleep as if he's dreaming about something astonishing. I go to sleep and don't dream anything at all.

When we wake up, my mom's surprised that we're here, since she thought we were supposed to be at Colby's house, but she's in a really good mood. She always is, right when she's finished a painting.

"You wouldn't *believe* how late I stayed up," she says, not realizing that Colby and I were up even later. "Waffles or eggs?"

Later, we sit around eating, then Colby asks to see her new painting, and not just because he's polite to grown-ups (which he is). He likes all of my mom's paintings, even the weird ones.

Actually, this one isn't bad.

"UFO patterns in a muddy field?" asks Colby. Mom tilts her head as if she's considering that. I just stand there and laugh.

My mom is not like other moms. That's because she's an artist.

Sometimes it's really fun having an artist for a mom. She lets me use her paints, even the smelly ones you're not supposed to get on your skin. Oil paints. They come in tubes, like toothpaste. I love their names!

Most colors are poisonous, so I'm very careful. Sometimes, I work on my own paintings. Right now, I'm doing one of dots. They're all different colors and sizes, from berries to beach balls. Once, I made a pretty good painting of Tofu, which is hard since he doesn't sit still unless he's sleeping. So I did him running. It's kind of a blur, but you can tell it's Tofu. My mom saved it. She saves all my art. It's a good thing we have such a big house. There are canvases stacked *everywhere*.

But sometimes I wish Mom had an ordinary job. She could work in an office or sell shoes or be a lawyer. Here's why:

There's a breast on our living room wall. It's made of plaster. Mom won't ever take it down because it's *her* breast. She made the sculpture of it before she lost the real one. She had to have it removed because of cancer.

"This was before you arrived on the scene,"

my mom explains when we talk about it. "I was very sick, but now I'm better."

On the side without a breast she has a long scar. I tell her she's like one of those archers from the Greek myths—those ladies who cut off one of their breasts so they could shoot their bows and arrows better. I read about them.

"Honey, that's an ancient rumor. I'm sure the Amazons could aim just fine with both breasts." But she laughs. She can joke about it now that she doesn't have cancer anymore. Her bra has a fake breast in it, so people can't tell. Her swimsuit does, too. When you squeeze the fake breast, it feels a bit wobbly. Like Jell-O. She could go to the hospital to add a new breast to her body, but she doesn't want to. "Enough surgery," she says, and that's that.

When I was little, Mom always told me not to worry—that I would have *two* breasts when I grew up. Not that I wanted breasts. Then or now. I don't even really like talking about breasts, but that's unavoidable since I'm in fourth grade.

Amanda has breasts, even though she's only ten. They stick out of her shirt. She looks all happy about it, but I wouldn't be. A breast on the living room wall is enough for me.

And sometimes, too much.

People see it up there.

Colby is okay with it, probably because he's a guy. I remember the first time he saw it.

"What's that?"

"Um . . . what?"

"That white thingy on the wall." He points. "That sculpture."

"That's my mom's breast."

"Ha. What's it doing on the wall?"

"Not her *real* breast, dummy."

"What's it for?"

"To remind her that she once had it, I guess."

"It looks funny."

"I know. Shut up."

I think we were about seven. Since then we haven't talked about it again. Besides, Colby understands art. Art is *supposed* to make you think. It's not just about pretty pictures.

Mostly, it's grown-ups who comment. (Maybe because I don't invite all that many kids into my living room.) My mom's friend Liza says, "Rosemary, honey, you're the strongest person I know." Liza always says that while standing right in front of the breast. It's on the wall next to a landscape and a photo of me back when I was a baby.

This morning, the man who comes to fix the sink that's been dripping forever sees the breast. He catches me looking at him looking at it. Instantly, he turns red in the face. I stare back at him and frown in a mature fashion.

Why do breasts make people act funny? What if Mom put a plaster cast of her nose or her foot on the wall? Would it be different?

Breasts are nothing but body parts.

They can be different sizes, like other body parts, I guess.

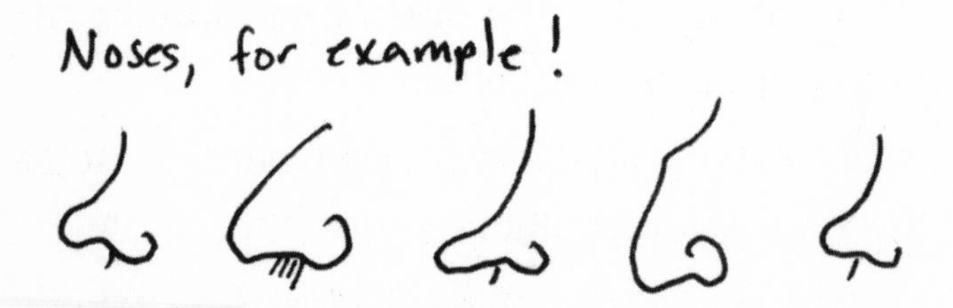

All bodies are different.

Mine is Chinese. That's very normal in China, but in Wolfgang, I'm the only one. Everybody knows I'm adopted. It's *obvious*. Sarah and Matt in my grade are adopted, too, but you can't tell by looking at them. They both have blue eyes, like the rest of their family.

Somewhere, far away in China, I have a birth mom. Unless she died. Another dad, too. Maybe. My mom says the orphanage has a record of my birth mother but not my birth dad. When I'm in high school and Mom has saved up enough money, we're going to go to China. It's so far away that when it's day here, it's night there.

I don't know if I want to go.

I don't even speak Chinese.

What if my birth mom wants to talk to me and I can't say anything?

Not that my birth mother would want to talk to me. She gave me away.

"She was so young, India," says Mom, who is of course glad about it, otherwise she wouldn't have me.

It's all so confusing. I don't tell anybody, but I'm very mad at my birth mother. If she doesn't want me, I don't want her. Sometimes I hide my face under my pillow and scream, "I don't want to be Chinese anymore!"

Why can't EVERYbody in Wolfgang be Chinese (instead of nobody)?

I don't even like egg-drop soup.

So who am I, anyway?

"I can't remember anything about the orphanage," I complain to Mom.

"That's normal," Mom says. "Nobody can really remember that far back. You were just a baby."

But the thing is, I have a secret. I *do* remember something. It's the color red. My memory about China is bright red, also gold. If we do go on a trip to Guangdong Province, where I was born, I'm going to be looking for it. Whatever it is, I'll know it when I see it.

For now, we're not going to China. We're off to Portland. Mom exhibits work in a gallery there. We're driving a new show to the city. Mom and me and Colby, since I'm allowed to take a friend as long as it's Colby.

"He's my assistant," says Mom, and I would be jealous, but Colby deserves the title more than I do, since he actually *wants* the job! Not only that, when he helps load her work in and out of the car, he's very, very careful. I'm not that careful, but I do love a trip to Portland. It takes a few hours to get there. Colby and I sit in the back and count stuff. One time, we saw eighty-seven cows. Another time we saw two moose. This time we see something spectacular: one enormous hot-air balloon.

"You and Colby can help me unload," says Mom, as if we didn't know the plan. "Then we'll go for lunch in the city."

We start out on a sunny morning, but by the time we get down there, it's foggy. You can even hear the foghorns. When I was little, I called them frog horns.

"It's often foggy by the sea," says Mom, who grew up on the coast. Portland isn't a very big city, but to me, it looks huge. From the highway you can see a lot of buildings. Some of them are pretty tall. They probably have elevators. There isn't a single elevator in all of Wolfgang.

The art gallery is on the ground floor of a building in the Old Port part of Portland. Mom and Colby lug the paintings while I open the doors. I recognize the gallery owner. She has short hair and enormous glasses.

"Oh, Rosemary," she says, swaying on her tiptoes. "These are beautiful."

"I especially like the one with the spirals," comments Colby, who isn't shy about his art opinions. "It's as wild as my baby sister." Knowing Monica, I agree with him. The gallery lady laughs. I can tell she thinks Colby is adorable, but Colby isn't noticing. He's walking around looking at the other artists' work on the walls. There's some crazy stuff in here.

After my mom and the big-glasses lady talk for a while, we go to lunch. Just the three of us. Mom takes us to Ruby Fong's. It's a new Chinese restaurant not that far from the gallery. The inside is red and gold and that makes me happy, too. When we sit down, a tall Chinese man comes over to take our order, but we say we're all going to have the buffet. That way, we can pick and choose. They have many kinds of food, even mashed potatoes, which I don't think are very Chinese. I load my plate with lo mein.

"Show me how to use chopsticks again," says Colby. And I do. I can do *some* Chinese things, even if my American mom taught me.

I smile at the waiter when he comes to take our empty plates. Suddenly, I ask him, "What does red mean in China?"

He smiles back at me. "Red is very lucky in China." He gives us each a fortune cookie. Fortune cookies aren't really Chinese, says Mom. They were invented in America. People *think* they're Chinese. This reminds me of me. I'm from China but I was a different person

You never know what you're going to get!

there. My name wasn't even India. It was Fei, which is now my middle name. So now I'm an American invention.

I open my cookie. It says, "You will have many wonderful adventures." I eat up the whole cookie, even though it tastes like sugary cardboard. You *have* to do that, if you want the fortune to come true, at least that's what we say. Colby reads his fortune: "There is hard work to be done." He doesn't eat his. Mom holds up her slip of paper. "Good luck will come to you from far across the sea."

She smiles at me. "It already has," she says.

I love my mom. And I'm thinking my heart probably looks exactly the same as hers—red, strong, and happy.

The human heart is complicated and simple at the same time!

4
The Snake Mistake

I love my dad, too, except that he lives with Richard, and I'm just not so sure about Richard. It doesn't seem fair that he gets to see Dad every day and I don't, and I've known Dad all my life. Today, they are coming to take me to Camden, which is about a zillion-mile drive, even in a fancy sports car. The good thing is, they say I can bring a friend, and of course I choose Colby. His mom says he can go.

"It's great timing," Colby reminds me, since Saturday is everyone-clean-the-house day at

Colby's. For some reason, Mom and I never have those. We have a huge house with only two people and one dog, so it swallows up the clutter and mess pretty well (except for Tofu's fur when he sheds, and that's most of the time). Colby has a tiny house with six kids, two grown-ups, and three cats, so they all have to pitch in.

"Don't worry," yells his brother Jacob when Dad and Richard and I swing by in the Mitsubishi Spider to pick Colby up. "We'll save you the bathrooms." I think he's kidding, but Colby says he's not.

We drive east toward Camden and the sea without saying much. This is because Dad and Richard are in the front seat and they've got the radio on. They always listen to National Public Radio, and there's a lot of really calm talking about sometimes awful things, and occasionally jazz. Colby and I don't talk much either, since it's still early and Colby is always sleepy until about noon, even in school. It's like he comes to life in the afternoon. We do look for cool things, but mostly it's cows and hills and trees, and nothing much sticks out.

"Isn't it lovely to see new leaves?" Richard turns around to us and says in his German accent. I suppose he's right since winter lasts so long around here, but I merely nod. He's making an effort, as my Mom might say, but that doesn't mean I have to.

"Yes, it is," says Colby, since he knows how to be polite in his sleep.

Once, I asked him about growing up in Stuttgart, and he was so happy... I do make an effort sometimes.

The miles go by. We stop at a gas station and use the toilets. Dad lets us buy candy bars, which is unusual, especially since I know he has carrot sticks and pretzels for us in the car. He likes to be well prepared, so he travels with snacks. I choose Snickers, like I always do, and Colby settles on a bag of sour Skittles. He always takes a long time to decide.

When we walk back to the car, Dad puts his arm around me and I smell his familiar smell, combined with a slight dash of gas station restroom disinfectant odor. He's my dad and I love him, but I just wish he were still all mine.

"We'll go up Mount Battie," he says, giving my shoulder a little squeeze. "Remember when you and I camped there and that falcon swooped down?" How could I forget? It was only last summer. I grin up at him even though I know that, with Richard along, we'll be *driving* up, not hiking. The mountain has car access and Richard only has fancy, shiny shoes . . . nothing you could go up a muddy trail in. He's not a man who moves much, as far as I can tell. It's like he lives only in his brain.

And some people
stay mostly in their heads . . .

Like Mrs. O
(in a nice way)
MOZART

and Richard—
who knows what he's thinking?

The land starts to flatten out. Then, in the distance, we see the Camden Hills. We come over a rise, and there it is—the wide old sea. It sparkles at us. A single early-season boat sails toward the horizon. It makes me happy, all of a sudden, like there are possibilities out there I've never thought of. (And also Portugal. It's across the sea from Maine, if you travel a long, long way.)

"We'll have a lovely late lunch at the restaurant where Richard and I met," says my dad, "but first, let's go up Mount Battie."

I don't actually know if I care where Richard and my dad met. We drive through Camden, with its much-fancier-than-Wolfgang shops. It's pretty quiet since it's not tourist season yet. In the summer, it's crazy busy with people who want to buy lighthouse keychains, and there's nothing wrong with that. I have one myself since I'm an inland girl and I come to Camden every year with my dad. Some people in Maine don't like tourists, but I do. If you can't visit the world, then why not let it come to you? Besides, there aren't really any tourists in Wolfgang. I guess there's not much to visit if you don't love streams and fields. Our one big attraction is the Civil War cannon in the middle of town.

Most of the time, someone has stuffed an empty can into it, instead of recycling...

so Colby and I call it the SODA CANNON (which is funny if you have our sense of humor).

We're about to wind up the mountain road when I make my big discovery. Colby has packed his rubber snake, Zelda. I see her fanged mouth hanging out of his backpack. He's had Zelda ever since I met him. She's about two feet long and rather convincing, if you don't know anything about snakes.

When we were little, I'd bring my stuffed dinosaurs and Colby would bring Zelda and we'd set up little towns for them, with houses made of paper. They were very civilized reptiles except when they were at war with each other. Then they'd rip up all their paper houses and we'd have to start building all over again, but that was half the fun. When Colby did Zelda's voice, he'd get all s-s-slithery. It's been a long time since we played that game. Still, I'm glad to see Zelda. She gives me an idea.

"Can I borrow her?" I ask Colby. "Just until lunch?"

He shrugs. "Sure."

I wonder why he brought her in the first place, but I don't ask. I don't want to draw *any* attention to her now that we're all getting out of the car at the top of the mountain. I wind her into a tight little ball and stuff her in my pocket. She mostly fits.

There's a fire tower up here, and no other people, and it's amazing because of the long, long view. You can see the whole town of Camden. It looks like a photograph, with little houses, and churches, and tiny cars. Those tiny specks are people! And, of course, we can see the sea.

Richard sits down at the base of the tower and looks solemnly out over everything, as if he might say something important about it. Or not. Richard isn't a big talker. My dad sits down for a moment, too, then gets up and wanders all around the rocky mountaintop. He's not a sitting-still kind of person. Colby walks around with me and Zelda the Hidden. We find a path through some low bushes. It takes us to a great lookout point. I don't even have to tell Colby my plan—he already knows because he's been my friend forever.

"Do you really think he'll fall for it?"

"Yup."

"Do you really think it's a good idea?"

I don't answer that one, since I'm not sure.

I just put Zelda on the path, in a very natural, snaky-looking way, then I get Dad and Richard, and tell them that the view is *much* better from over here.

"You can even see the lake we swam in last summer," I say, and act very jolly. "Megunticook. It's *so* blue."

It works even better than I hoped it would, and that's the problem. Richard goes first. Richard sees Zelda on the path and thinks she's a real snake. Richard actually kind of yelps and clutches at his chest. Dad takes Richard's arm for a moment and leans down to pick up Zelda. Dad doesn't laugh, like I thought he would. Maybe he recognizes Zelda from long ago.

"In my country," says Richard, sitting down on a rock, breathing a bit funny, "there are *vipers*." He says *vipers* with a hissing *s,* but that's probably because he's German. "When I was a small boy, I was very afraid."

"Don't be afraid," I say too loudly. "It's only *rubber*." Then I realize that Dad might think Colby planned this trick, and since he didn't, I have to say it. The word I don't love to say, especially to Richard.

"Sorry."

"Ah," says Richard. "You were having a little joke, yes?" He looks normal again, but Dad has frown lines on his face.

We drive down the mountain and go out to the place where Richard and Dad met, which turns out to serve mostly seafood and is really fancy. Mom would make *observations* if she saw all the white napkins and tablecloths.

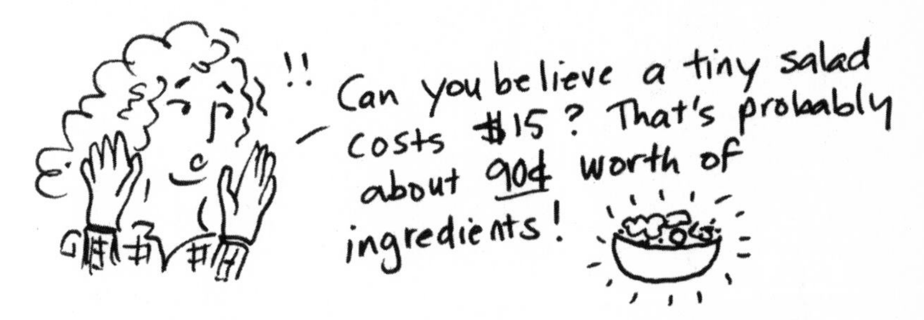

(Mom's more of a potluck type of person.)

She can get very worked up about things like this, so it's a good thing she's not here, for a lot of other reasons, too. Thinking about her, I feel slightly better. Maybe she wouldn't put a rubber snake on a path, but she'd probably put her foot in her mouth and then regret it.

Richard and Dad seem to be having a lovely time, and Colby gets to order a whole lobster for himself, so he's in heaven. It's very hard to eat a lobster on a white tablecloth, but Colby does it without squirting much lobster juice on everything. I pick at my chowder. I'm surprised I didn't order a lobster, since I love them, but I wasn't in a good-enough mood. I probably shouldn't have tried to scare Richard. Not ordering lobster was my secret punishment for myself.

But Richard offers me the part of his chocolate cake he just can't eat because he says he's stuffed, so I guess he isn't too mad at me. It's actually delicious and I am not that full, even though I just ate my entire ice-cream sundae with extra whipped cream. (I don't usually punish myself too hard.)

"Good thing the dessert stomach is a different stomach," says my dad, smiling. That's one of his old lines. I've heard it about fifty-two times, but I still smile.

On the way home, Dad doesn't turn on the radio. Instead, we all play Twenty Questions. I stump everybody by thinking of a manatee. Zelda is safely back in Colby's backpack with only the tip of her tail sticking out. When we slow down through all the little towns between Camden and Wolfgang, people wave as we go by. I think it's because they like the look of our extra-snazzy sportscar, but maybe we just look happy.

5 Richard's Big Surprise

Dad and Richard live in Ottenbury, in a place called The Pines. It's condos. There's not a single kid in The Pines, except sometimes me, and there are also hardly any pines. The Pines does not allow dogs or cats, so when I visit, Tofu stays at home with Mom and makes messes because he misses me so much. I miss him, too.

Ottenbury's not all that far from Wolfgang, but to get there you take very twisty roads. I sometimes get carsick if I have to sit in the back. That's why I love it when my dad comes to pick me up *without* Richard. He lets me sit in the front. This makes Mom mad.

"It's not safe," she always says. "And he's a *doctor*. He should know better."

Well, at least I don't get carsick in front. I'm especially glad if he's driving his Mini Cooper. It's just my size, and it's my favorite color: red. That's Dad's favorite color, too. We joke that we're going to play chess on the cute black-and-white checkered roof, but we never do.

My dad and Richard have five cars for only *two* people. My mom thinks this is excessive.

"How completely decadent," she says, every single time I go visit.

She might be right about that, but I get tired

of her always criticizing my dad, so I don't agree. Besides, their cars are cool.

"They *collect* cars," I inform her. "It's an investment." I think maybe she's jealous, but she says those sorts of things aren't important to her at all. She says she needs space for her canvases and for me, of course, and her old Subaru works just fine except when it's in the shop.

"We'll chalk it up to philosophical differences," she says when she hears about their latest (the Alfa Romeo).

"You just have different taste," I remind her.

"You can say that again, sweetie," Mom replies, but I don't.

So, this particular weekend, Dad comes to pick me up with no Richard, and I think it's going to be a *great* weekend. He says we're taking a hike, and hiking is *not* one of Richard's hobbies in the least. I'm happy that it's going to be just the two of us, like it hardly ever is anymore.

Sometimes things don't turn out the way you want.

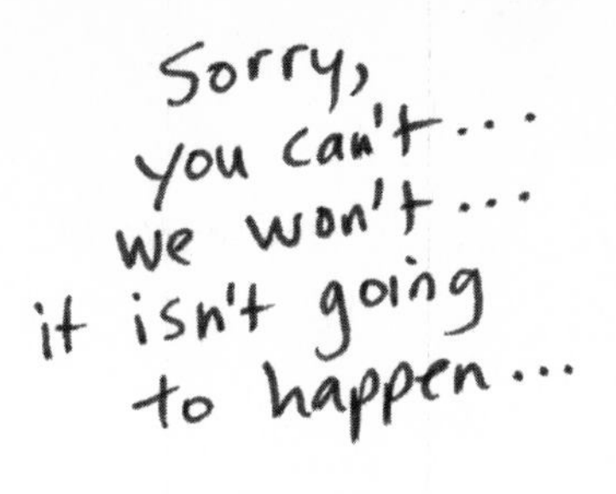

Especially at my dad's. Maybe it's because I'm always hoping too hard when I'm with him.

The first thing that happens is that I get up on Saturday and my dad isn't even *there*. Richard is cooking special pancakes (called crêpes) in the kitchen, in his stiff, silent way. I do like crêpes, though, so I go sit near him. He's a very precise cook, even when he's using lots of eggs. There's not even any splatter. He puts Nutella on each perfect pancake and rolls it up. I have to admit it smells good.

"French children often eat chocolate on their baguettes," he says. He's told me this a few times already. Grown-ups repeat themselves a lot.

"Where's Dad?" I ask casually, hoping he's out getting more orange juice or something.

"I'm sorry, India," he says. "Your father had to go into the office. The doctor on call woke up sick and he had to take her place." He gives a little sigh. Maybe he's sad that Dad isn't around on a weekend, or maybe he's already annoyed that he's stuck with me. I roll my eyes, but not so he can see me. No Dad. No camping. Just me and Richard. He'll either ignore me or give me coloring books or something, as if I'm about six.

"He left you this note," Richard says, almost like an afterthought.

Dear Indy,

So sorry we won't have our hiking weekend, but I know Richard wants to take you out for a SURPRISE! Have fun and see you for supper. We can make PIZZA!

Love! xox Dad

I look at Richard. "What's the surprise?"

Richard strokes his beard the way he almost always does before he says anything. "If I tell you, where is the surprise?" Then he smiles shyly and adds, "We're going shopping, you and I."

I wrinkle my nose. I hate shopping, especially the grocery kind. It usually takes forever.

"Shopping for someone special," he adds. I wonder if that's supposed to mean me.

"Okay," I say, shrugging my shoulders. I don't add "whatever," but that's how I feel. The weekend is ruined. I might as well go shopping. After that, we could clean the kitchen. Not that it needs it. At Richard and Dad's house, you could perform surgery in any room (but mine), it's so clean.

Richard nods at me, looking pleased with himself. "You'll like this," he adds. Personally, I hate when people tell me I'll like something. How would they know? Mind reading isn't for real.

At least it better not be.

We stack the dishes in the sink and get into the car. It's the Alfa Romeo, Richard's special vehicle, and I guess I should feel honored, but it's too cold to put the top down, so instead I feel annoyed. Sometimes my mom tells me I forget to think about others and that I'm not a charitable person. But I don't care.

Outside, I look like the normal me, but I'm not smiling. Even after a whole year, I don't know Richard well enough to sulk in front of him, and that's kind of weird, not to mention inconvenient, too. A person should be able to sulk in her own home, even if it's not the one she usually lives in!

We drive through town and over a bridge, not talking at all. After a few minutes we pull up to a long white building. The sign says BURT'S FARM AND FEED. I've never been here before. Richard holds the door open for me with a little bow, and we walk in. It's busy. There are rows and rows of potting soil and other gardening things, and people standing in line with bags of birdseed and chew toys. The place smells of hay. Richard takes me to the back of the store. There's a whole wall of fish for sale, swimming in their own little aquarium worlds, and shy small animals like guinea pigs hiding under the shavings in their cages. I want to look at a rabbit, but Richard takes me by the shoulder with his pinchy hand and steers me into a small room. It's all twittery in there.

And that's the first time I ever see her: Bird.

Cockatiel of the Universe.

Instantly, I love her.

We take her home in a brand-new

cage. I sit in the back holding it. I don't feel carsick at all. Richard turns on the radio to the classical station.

"We'll have to get her whistling Mozart," he explains.

When we get back to The Pines, the nosy neighbor I've never met but I always see is in her driveway. She's the kind of person with perfect hair and lipstick who does not approve of anybody else in the whole world. She looks at me as I carefully take Bird out of the car.

"You must be Andrew and Richard's little girl," she says with an eager look in her eyes. Maybe she thinks it's odd that Dad and Richard are together like a couple. A lot of people do. But Bird is here and I have more important things on my mind, so I calmly blink and say, "Yes, I am." I lug the cage up the front steps. Richard is holding the door open for me.

I think I might be charitable after all.

6

Amanda Roden Is Not Perfect

I do not stay charitable for long.

One of the reasons I hate Amanda Roden is she's such a *girl*. I'm a girl, too, of course, but I'm not that kind of girl. Like last Thursday, I was walking by on the other side of the street, since I *never* walk on the sidewalk right next to her house. She was out there doing cartwheels all over the place, showing off as usual. Jacob was there with her. He's one of Colby's brothers and he's okay, but he's a lot older than we are. Sixth grade. That's why he's cool enough for

Amanda to hang out with. So, Miss Cartwheel Queen stops doing cartwheels and I can tell she sees me.

"Hey, India!" yells Jacob, but Amanda doesn't say anything. I give the world's smallest wave, to Jacob only, and keep walking. Then I hear Amanda, in a totally loud voice, say, "Do you know any girls who like spiders?" She's flicking something out of her hair. "Ew, gross." It's probably a leaf, although I hope it's an ultrasticky spiderweb.

The thing is, I'm really into spiders and she knows it. I brought in my collection in third grade. There were a lot of little, dead dry spiders and one big live wolf spider with fat, hairy legs. I let that one go, practically the same day. He was a bit too jumpy. My teacher last year, Mrs. Gerber, thought it was great, but Amanda didn't. Even back when she wasn't totally evil she made it clear that she didn't want to even *look* at poor Wolfie.

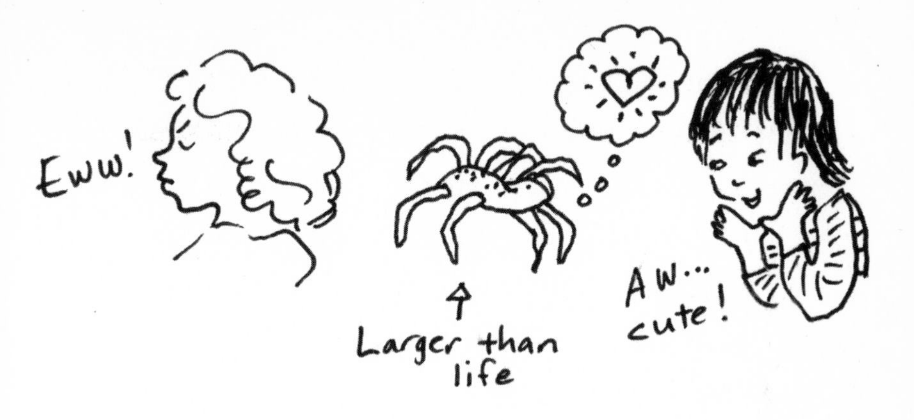

Obviously, she's saying that spider thing to get to me, and so Jacob will laugh and protect her from some poor innocent daddy longlegs on her front lawn. Daddy longlegs aren't even technically spiders. It's totally pathetic. I wish a dozen amazing arachnids would spin webs in the Rodent's yard and that she'd walk straight into them. It wouldn't be great for the spiders, I guess, but they're used to rebuilding. She'd be just another natural disaster to them.

I try to ignore the Rodent, and it's almost easy. I'm on my way to meet Colby. We're going up into the tree—that's why I don't have Tofu with me, since he'd give us away. It's the crab apple on the corner of Main and Elm, at the edge of the pharmacy parking lot. It's a great tree. First of all, it has low branches, so you can get up in it pretty easily. At this time of year, it's thick with blossoms (and bees), so nobody can see you unless they know you're there. But you can see them through the gaps.

Passersby walk right under you, so you can hear anything they might be saying. It's a great way to spy on people. "It might rain later" is usually about as interesting as it gets, but it still feels all secret and cool up there. And perfumey, from all the blossoms.

When I get to the tree, Colby's already up in the branches. I know because his bike is leaning on the far fence. The trick is climbing up without anybody noticing. In a town as quiet as this one, it's not that hard. I wait while two cars pass, then I pull myself up onto the lowest branch.

"Hey, India," Colby says from above.

"I saw your brother at the Rodent's house," I tell him. He shrugs. He doesn't ask which brother, though, so I figure it isn't the first time *she's* hung out with Jacob. Colby and I sit there for a long time, not saying much. The wind swishes in the trees. The fire engine roars by with its siren on. Finally, some innocent victims come by. It's Mrs. Snow from the bank. My mom always says hi to her. Mrs. Snow and somebody else. The somebody else is talking, right as the two ladies walk three feet under our very noses. They don't look up. Hardly anybody does look up. It almost makes me feel sorry for the sky.

". . . and then he told me that anybody who ate pickled herring was his kind of person. So, we have . . ." and then we can't hear any more. They walk fast, for oldish ladies.

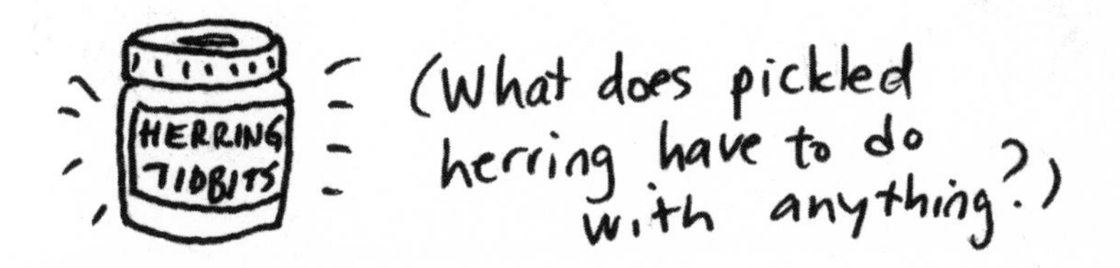

Right when we're about to climb back down because it's so boring, who should come strolling down the street but the Rodent. She's got her sidekick, Melanie, with her. Melanie's okay, except when she's anywhere near Amanda, and then she becomes instantly annoying. They're whispering, as if they're talking about something secret, even though nobody else is around.

Except us.

They stop right under our tree! Colby looks at me, and I look at him. We're both absolutely quiet, even though a big, fat laugh is trying to burst itself out of me. Colby, too. I can tell by looking at him, which I'm trying not to do. I hardly breathe.

"It's not my fault," Amanda giggles. "I only did it because they did."

"That's right," Melanie agrees. Of course she'd agree with anything the Rodent said.

"Finders keepers, losers weepers," Amanda snickers.

"Definitely," says Melanie. "It's yours now."

"This will totally get the police on me, though," laughs the Rodent.

"I know it," squeals Melanie, who lets Amanda put her arm around her but doesn't quite dare put hers around Amanda. That's because Melanie by herself isn't really that popular.

"The *police*?" says Colby when we can't see them anymore.

We jump out of the tree and just stand there, looking at each other. "Now what?" I say, thinking we have some serious detective work to do.

"I think I'll go home for dinner," Colby says, and that sounds like the dumbest idea I've ever heard until I remember that he has two brothers and three sisters so there will be a lot of talking. Maybe one of them knows something. Jacob, for instance. He was hanging out with the main suspect, after all. Now all we have to do is figure out the crime.

I go home to eat with Mom and Tofu, or possibly just Tofu if Mom's stuck in a painting again.

Sometimes I wish I had a big family, too. "Call me when you get done," I tell him as he rides off.

"Okay," says Colby. "See ya later."

But after dinner, he doesn't call and neither do I. Once in a while, I feel shy and that's really weird. Colby's been my friend since we both wore diapers, but now that we're in fourth grade, people say stupid stuff. "How's your handsome boyfriend?" asks my otherwise very nice neighbor Mrs. Ordinance. And I can't stand that. He's *not* my boyfriend! He's just my *friend*. But I still get embarrassed. I decide to sit in my beanbag chair and read. Tofu loves it when I do that because I usually have popcorn. But what I'm really doing is thinking.

At ten, my mother comes to tell me she's figured out how the color orange is going to work in her new piece and to please turn my light off. Good thing it's not a school night. But I can't sleep. It's too hot, especially for May. Tofu keeps snoring, and my mind's whirring. I spend a long time not being able to sleep, until I finally get up and go sit on our porch swing. Tofu wakes up instantly and comes with me. That dog can go from the deepest dream to wide awake in one second.

The street's quiet. Everything looks different at night. Sometimes it looks scary, but tonight it looks magical. The air is purple and soft, and the foggy sky comes almost down to the ground.

I walk around in the wet grass in my nightgown. There's a light on next door, even though I'm pretty sure it's after midnight. Mrs. Ordinance doesn't always sleep well. "Too many memories" is what she's told me. I guess they're the sad kind. Still, I'm glad that somebody else is up.

Night is a different world.

Then I hear it.

First, I think it might be a little lost kitten, but Tofu would have found it by now. He likes to play with cats, even though they aren't always thrilled. But it's not an animal. It's a person and the person is crying.

I creep over to the window and stand on my toes, trying to see. It's Mrs. Ordinance herself, which doesn't surprise me, since she lives alone and hardly ever has visitors except me and her bridge club. She's hunched over her kitchen table and her shoulders rise up and sag down. This isn't crying, it's sobbing, and I don't know what to do. Tofu doesn't either, so he starts howling, and before I know it, Mrs. Ordinance is wiping her eyes and opening the window to look.

I don't want to run off and creep her out, so she sees us. "Sorry, Mrs. Ordinance. I couldn't sleep." That doesn't explain why I'm looking in her window, of course. Tofu wags his tail. When he sees Mrs. O, he thinks of cookies.

"Oh, honey," says Mrs. Ordinance. "I can't sleep either. Maybe you could come in for some hot milk, then we could both try again."

If it was anybody else, I'd have to wake Mom and tell her. But it's Mrs. O. She's practically my aunt.

"Okay," I say. Tofu comes too. He's always invited to Mrs. O's house.

We sit up drinking hot milk (not as bad as it sounds) and eating oatmeal cookies. For a person who lives alone, she sure does a lot of baking.

"I'm upset, India," Mrs. O explains. That's what I love about her. She talks to me as if I'm her friend, not just a kid. "I have lost my purse. Sometime yesterday." Her wrinkled face looks tired. "Downtown." She sighs. "It's not the bag I care about, or even my wallet and the money. But my photos, India, all my photos."

She's shown me those photos more than once. She's always looking at them. They're pictures of her mother and father and sister, people who aren't alive anymore. I think they died in some kind of war. Her husband's in there, too. He had a heart attack a long time ago. I never met him. She keeps the photos in her wallet so they'll always be close to her.

"I asked the police to look, but what can I do?" she says. "I'm merely an old lady with a lost purse. They have bigger cases to crack." I think for a minute. This is Wolfgang. *What bigger cases?*

"It'll be okay, Mrs. O," I say. "Let's get to bed and we'll work on it in the morning." I put my arm around her, the way Amanda did with Melanie, and it hits me: There could be a connection here.

The next morning, which is only a few hours later, I'm out of bed and out of the house before breakfast. I have to talk to Colby. I think Amanda found the purse. Didn't she say something about "finders keepers"? And the loser is definitely weeping.

Colby isn't awake, though. He likes to sleep. I like to sleep, too, but not when I'm involved in a major criminal case.

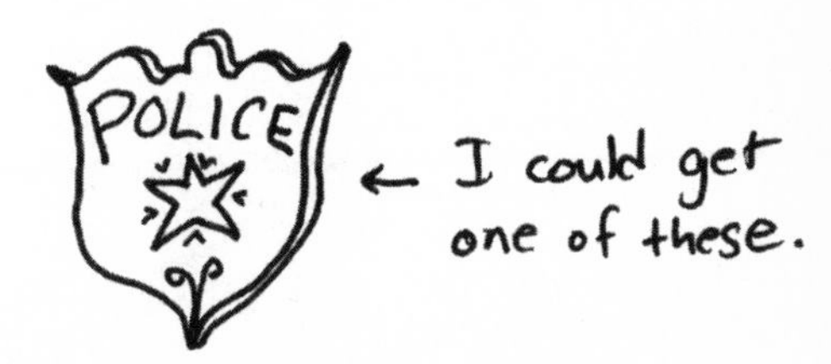

"You and I are going to the police, Tofu," I tell my trusty assistant. "They've got to know."

That's how I find myself walking into the police station. I remember coming here on a second-grade field trip. The officer at the desk is George's mom. George is in my class. His mother smiles at me. "India," she says, "what brings you here?"

"I think I know who stole Mrs. Ordinance's purse!" I blurt out. Before I can yell "Amanda Roden," George's mom interrupts me.

"What lovely timing you have, India." She smiles at me. "The purse was turned in this morning. The custodian at the library found it in their parking lot. He would have brought it over to Mrs. Ordinance herself, but he was on his way to visit his daughter in New Hampshire." She continues smiling at me, as if this is the best news in the world, and it is good news, but also bad news, because I'm wrong.

"Do you want me to call Mrs. Ordinance to see if she'd like you to bring it to her?"

I nod. And when Tofu and I walk in Mrs. O's door fifteen minutes later, I do feel sort of heroic. Mrs. O gives me a great big hug. She immediately opens the purse and hands me a dollar, but I don't take it.

"It's okay, Mrs. O," I say. "I didn't find your purse. I don't need a reward."

Dollars are nice, but I don't deserve one. I'm not really a hero—I'm a loser. I was about to turn Amanda in, and she didn't have anything to do with this.

Later on, when I'm sulking in the tree all by myself, who should walk by like a bad rerun? Melanie and Amanda. The Rodent's all decked out in some kind of sparkly, low-cut, glamorous supermodel shirt.

"I *love* it, Amanda," gushes Melanie. "Even if you took it from the junior high school lost and found."

"I don't know," says the Rodent. "Does it make me look fat?"

"No way," says Melanie.

"It's so sparkly," the Rodent giggles. "I'll probably get arrested by the fashion police!"

They keep walking and giggling, and it's a lucky thing that I don't fall out of the tree from the stupidity of it all. The *fashion* police? How could she be so dumb?

Later, I ask my mom about the fashion police. "Who are they, exactly?"

"Oh, honey." Mom laughs. "They're not real police. That's just an expression. It means if your friends or acquaintances tell you you're wearing something unsuitable."

How could *I* be so dumb?

7

Tofu's Early-Morning Adventure

I wake up before five o'clock on the first day of June. It's Saturday. I don't actually have to get up, since Dad isn't coming until later. Colby and his family are away for the weekend—not that he'd be up. The clock says 4:45 a.m. Who gets up this early except for hunters and babies? Maybe fishermen. I try to go back to sleep but I can't. I realize why—it's Tofu. He's not on my bed. Not only that, he's howling, the way he does at the moon and all the squirrels he can't get and sometimes invisible whatevers. I race down the stairs. I don't want Mom to wake up. She's kind of a nutcase if she's been painting half the night and then has to get up early.

What my mom is capable of doing when she's a nutcase:

Burning toast!

Getting rubber bands stuck in her hair because she can't find her hair ties...

AND MUCH MORE !!!!

Tofu is out on the sunporch, howling away as if he has a deep, deep longing (or possibly a toothache).

"What is it?" I ask him, stroking his ears.

Of course he doesn't tell me. He does stop howling, but he's still squirming like crazy. I don't know whether to let him out (because that's what he wants) or not let him out (in case what he has a deep, deep longing for is a porcupine or a skunk).

I decide we'll go out together, with him on the leash. Tofu looks at me. If he could really talk, he'd say, "What *is* this strange object?" That's because we hardly ever have to put the leash on him.

The morning is still chilly, since the sun has only just begun to rise. A mist hangs over the lawn and hides the lilac bush. I can smell the lilacs, though, and it reminds me that summer is really coming. Even though there's no school, summer is one of my favorite times of year. There's more ice cream, for example. And adventures.

It is possible I'm about to go on an adventure right now.

Tofu leads the way. He's a dog with a purpose. First he sniffs the entire length of the garden, from the stone wall to the early tulips. Then he drags me to Mrs. O's house and smells everything over there, mostly her wheelbarrow and the front steps. He adds a little statement of his own on his favorite fire hydrant. Then he cocks his head like he's listening very hard, and we're off down Buckle Street so fast I have to run.

Dogs can smell better
than
people can see!

What Tofu can probably smell:

a candy wrapper
far away...

the trail
of a snail
on a blade
of grass...

hiding
mice...

... and worse things
(but he likes those).

Tofu keeps his nose down and leads us by all the sleepy houses. Now that I'm more awake, it's good to be up so early. The world is more private, like a painting that only Tofu and I are walking around in. Then a car drives down the street and the painting comes to life. It's a station wagon I've never seen before. A woman leans out the window and throws a newspaper onto the Andersons' porch. She skips the Rudwells' house but throws one onto Mrs. Ordinance's front steps. The lady's got wicked good aim and hardly even slows down to make the toss. She should probably play professional baseball or something. We wave at each other, then she's gone.

By now, we're at the end of the street, where Buckle turns into a dead end. It's the beginning of the big woods that pretty much surround Wolfgang in any direction you take. Tofu doesn't hesitate at all—he drags me on to wake up all the mosquitoes. All at once, I can hear it, too. The reason he's howling and pulling is a mysterious and faraway sound. It's beautiful and sad, like the call of the whale. (I have heard whale songs on a CD, not in person underwater, although that would be amazing.)

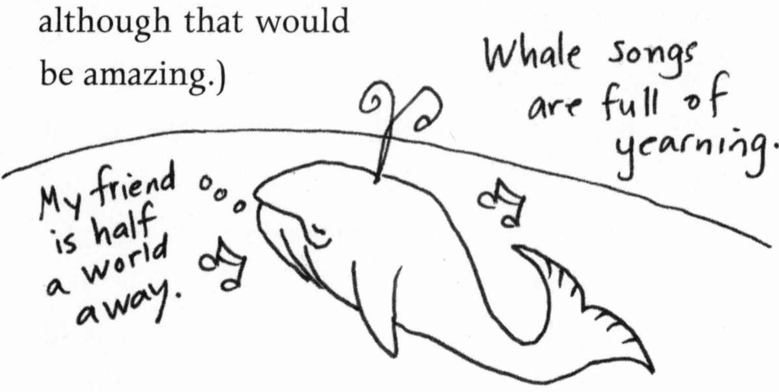

No wonder Tofu is bursting with excitement. He pulls me over roots and rocks. I try not to trip. Tofu can scamper, even when there is no path, but I'm not as talented.

I'm not really paying attention to where we're going, but that's okay, since Tofu has his nose. As long as I still have him on the leash, he'll take me home. He even knows the word, and if "home" doesn't work, I can always say "cookies" and he'll drag me to Mrs. O's house, and that's close enough.

The sound gets louder, but remains puzzling. Could it be a moose, moaning very musically?

"Tofu," I say, pulling us to a halt, "slow down. We have to sneak up on whatever this is." Tofu doesn't really understand "slow down," but I use all my muscle power and it works. Suddenly, I know what the strange sound is—a saxophone. But who would be playing it this early in the morning? I also know *where* the sound is coming from. The old quarry. It fills up with water in the spring and summer, but Mom says I'm not allowed to swim there, even though people do. There's a junked car under all the water. You can see it in the fall, when the water gets low.

Long ago, before I was born, a boy jumped in from the tall rocks and never came out. Mostly teens hang out there in the summer, but I think they gather at night, and probably don't play the saxophone.

We sneak up on the tallest rocks, and I see him. The person playing the lonely music has a scruffy beard and old clothes. He's sitting on a huge chunk of granite on the far side, overlooking the deep, green water. Tofu wags his tail. He wants to run down to meet the man who is making the sound. Tofu thinks *everybody* is a friend.

The man is playing his saxophone *w-a-a-y* better than Jenny Anderson plays hers in our school band, but that's not too hard. (I probably shouldn't say that since I'm only in chorus, but it's the truth.) The saxophone man leans his head back and out pours the amazing sound. His eyes are closed. That's a good thing, since even behind our boulder, I feel obvious. I hold Tofu's collar and just listen. The air smells like old campfire smoke and pine mist. The music echoes off the rocks and across the water. I can't go any closer because he's definitely a stranger, so I just hold Tofu's collar as tightly as I can, and wonder.

Who is this man and why is he playing in the old quarry, for nobody at all?

Deadly
Nightshade
NO! NO! NO!

You have to be very careful
and smart to survive in the wild.

At the exact moment that I decide we should sneak away, Tofu decides to join the band. He tilts his head back and lets out a long, mournful howl, followed by some impressive yelping. The saxophone man stops playing and looks around.

"Hey," he says. "Who's there?" His voice is friendly, but I don't answer since I'm too busy dragging my dog in the opposite direction from the one he wants to go in.

"Home," I say to Tofu. "Cookies!"

Tofu wags his tail at me (he is usually hungry, after all) and off we go. I run so fast I can barely breathe, and before I know it we're back on Buckle Street. I can hear the distant sound of the saxophone. I'm sorry I had to run away. At least he's playing again, whoever he is.

Buckle Street is beginning to stir. I wave at Mr. Anderson, who is picking the paper up off his porch. I almost tell him to wake Jenny so she can hear the magical music and get some playing tips, but it's like I have a secret I don't want to share. Besides, unless you're really listening for the sound of the sax, it's hard to hear it now. Someone on the next block is mowing the lawn way too early. Cars are out. There's even a distant chain saw. I hear Mrs. O grinding her morning coffee as I walk back by her house, and all the sounds are mixed into one sound soup, with many flavors.

When I get to our house, Mom's up and out on the sunporch. This surprises me, since she's not a morning person at all.

"Did you and Tofu take a walk?" she asks, looking at me over her mug of tea. I come up the steps, grinning a grin that says *What does it look like?* I'm not sure if I want to explain. She probably wouldn't like it if she knew that I let Tofu take me to the old quarry, where there was a man, even if he was talented.

Instead we make muffins with chocolate chips and don't say much. After breakfast, Mom decides to do some sketching and I join her. I want to see if I can *draw* music. Maybe that will be a way of telling her.

Later in the morning, when it feels like afternoon because I've been up so long, Dad comes to take me to his house. I'm so excited, since I've seen Bird only once since we got her, and she must miss me a lot. Dad's in the white convertible, so as we drive to Ottenbury I put on my red sunglasses and pretend I'm a movie star, with my hair whipping all over my face.

For lunch at the condo, we eat Dad's Amazing Homemade Chicken Soup without Richard. I pretend to be slightly disappointed that he's not there, because sometimes I am polite. The truth is, as long as Dad and Bird are here, I'm happy.

"Have you named her yet?" I ask.

"No," says Dad. "We're just calling her Bird for now. Maybe you can think of something?"

Bird walks adorably up and down my leg and picks at my sock. All kinds of names race through my head but none of them sound like her. Marcella? No. Daphne? No. Lina? Lainey? Lolly? Nope nope nope!

"It's okay." Dad smiles. "Take your time. Maybe she'll tell you herself."

In the meantime, Dad shows me the pictures he took in Venice, since he finally made prints of them.

"This is the flooded piazza," he tells me. "Piazza San Marco. This is where I bought you that lovely striped blown glass."

And Venice looks really cool, the way there are so many bridges and canals. I hope it doesn't sink into the sea very fast, so I can go there, too. Someday.

Bird the Un-named sings along to the music on the radio, and there is a saxophone in it, and suddenly I want to tell my secret to Dad.

He listens very carefully, the way he always does. He doesn't tell me I shouldn't have gone down to the quarry. Instead, he nods thoughtfully and listens to the story of my early-morning mystery.

"Who was he?" I ask. "Where did he come from?"

Dad smiles and shrugs. "Not all who wander are lost," he says, getting up to do the dishes. That's a saying from J. R. R. Tolkien. We read all the *Lord of the Rings* books together last year.

While I wipe the table and Bird sings her

heart out back in her cage, I wonder where the saxophone man will play his music next and who will hear him.

Unheard music is different
from unsung songs or unpainted paintings.
It's more like how Venice exists
even if you've never been there,
or even heard of it.
It's still there!
It's still beautiful!

(Who said vases are boring?)

Venetian glass →
my dad
brought back for me.
He said I'd appreciate
it when I'm old, but

I ALREADY DO!

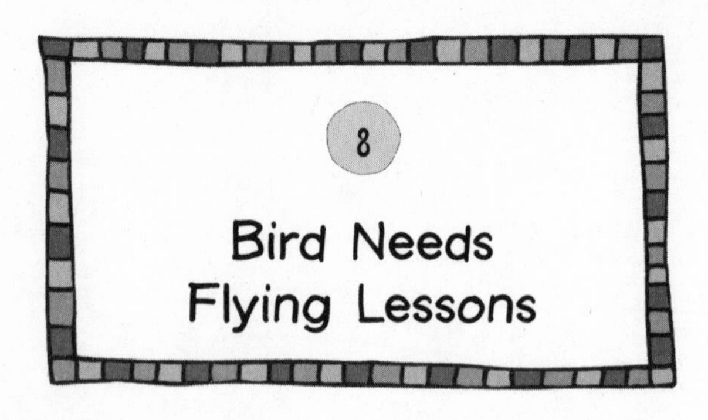

Two weeks later there's a disaster happening over at Dad and Richard's. It's about Bird. Bird is now called Beatrice Strawberry. It just came to me while I was walking home from school last week, and even Richard says it's the perfect name.

"She's a classic beauty," Richard says, "who deserves a classic name."

I figure the Strawberry part is like a middle name, and it's because she goes bananas for berries. If it turns out she's a boy (we forgot to ask), we can call her Benedict. Anyway, that's not the disaster. What's wrong is that the vet says Beatrice Strawberry is obese, as in very fat. We've been feeding her too much. She loves strawberries, and also Richard's crêpes. Who doesn't? But she's not supposed to be as puffy as she is. We all thought it was just her feathers. The thing is, she's so cute and happy when she eats, it's tempting to give her treats all day long.

"There are other ways to show love," says my mother when I tell her.

Anyway, my new weekend job is to exercise Beatrice. It's funny, having to do that for a creature with wings. I take her out of the cage and she tilts her head at me. The first time she hopped over to my finger, I was surprised by her claws. I'm used to them now.

"Here, chubby bird," I say, as I offer another

finger to her. The trick is to make her take a walk, from finger to finger. Over and over.

"Here, chubby bird," Beatrice says back to me. She's starting to talk a lot. Richard says that's because she's happy. Dad says that's because she's a tape recorder and it's a good thing she loves Ella Fitzgerald as much as he does.

"Tape recorders don't exist anymore," I tell him. "Everything's digital now." But it's true Beatrice Strawberry adores Ella Fitzgerald. Ella Fitzgerald sings about spring and love, and Beatrice whistles right along with her. It's really cute, but I guess singing alone in your cage is not enough exercise. So we have to do the finger walking thing.

One morning, I decide that finger walking is not enough. I'm going to let Beatrice out to fly. Richard said we might do that eventually, when Bird feels at home. I think she's ready. Anyway, Richard is away until suppertime, and Dad's out in his garden, since it's early June and that's where he's to be found these days. It's not a big garden, since this is condos, but everyone gets a few pots and planters to fill. What Dad wants are tomatoes. What I want is to exercise Beatrice, so I walk around the condo, making sure there aren't any open windows.

"Okay, Beatrice Strawberry Bird," I say. "It's time to fly." I lift her gently out of her cage and hold her up on my finger. I give her a little shake. She simply sits there and looks at me funny. Beatrice can give the evil eye. I give her another shake. "Shoo," I say. And, all of a sudden, Bird flies off toward a window. Her wings flutter so frantically that there's an actual breeze, but she's not so good at flying. She smacks into the window with a loud *thwomp,* falls to the floor, and lies there. Oh, no! I let Bird kill herself. I race over but Beatrice shakes her pretty self and takes off toward the mantel. Up there, she prances over all of Richard's fancy blown-glass pieces, then flutters crazily into the air. She's getting the hang of this flying business after all. I run around the room until I decide that she should come back and stop exercising. Sitting very quietly, I call her name.

"Beatrice. Beatrice Strawberry Bird!"

She calls back to me, "Bird!"

"Come here!" I order her.

"Here, chubby bird," says Beatrice, but it doesn't mean she's done with flying. She goes off through the door, into the kitchen. I follow, listening for her rustling.

But I can't find her anywhere.

"Bird?" I call. "Beatrice Strawberry!"

No answer.

"Treats," I say. "Pancakes, pancakes!"

No answer.

Outside the window, I can see Dad fussing with his tomato plants. I walk around the kitchen. It's crazy, but Bird is nowhere to be found. I decide to sit on a stool and wait. I sit there for quite a long time. At least ten minutes. Finally, I swallow my pride and slip out onto the little kitchen deck. I move fast so there's absolutely no way that Bird can follow me out into the world.

"Dad," I say.

"Hi, honey," he answers, looking up at me. Dad looks very happy when he's gardening. I'm not sure he's going to look happy for long.

"Um . . ." For some reason, it's hard to confess. I don't mind it when Mom scolds me, but I don't see Dad often enough. There's no time for him to be mad at me.

I just want him
to only love me!

"Is it time for lunch already?" He's still smiling.

"Well, no, it's just that I let Beatrice out of her cage and now I can't find her." All of that comes out really fast, before I can change my mind.

Dad stands up and strides toward the house. "Well," he says, but then he doesn't say anything else. He follows me in, sliding the deck door closed even faster than I did.

"Beatrice looked so bored," I say. "She needed more exercise."

Dad touches my shoulder. "It's Richard's bird, sweetie. You should have talked with him before you let her out. For now, let's just find her before he comes back, shall we?"

Fine with me.

But Dad can't find her either, even though I'm 95 percent sure that she has to be in the kitchen somewhere. We even look in the fridge. How many places could there be for a bird that big to hide?

Finally, we sit down and have leftovers. It's

Indian food and I love Indian food, but I'm not exactly hungry. Guilt and worry fill up my belly instead.

After lunch, I stay in the kitchen and read my book. It's about space-age pirates, but I can't concentrate.

"She's got to be somewhere," Dad says. He goes back outside.

Later in the afternoon, I hear Richard's Alfa Romeo zipping into the driveway. I see Dad and Richard talking. Richard's nodding his head. I feel like running up to my room and hiding, but I sit there. Beatrice Bird's still missing.

"I'm sorry," I say to Richard. "I thought she needed to fly."

Richard nods. "If I were a bird," he says, "where would I hide?" Richard is a very tall man, much taller than Dad. He lopes around the kitchen and stops in front of the fridge. On top of the fridge, pushed way back under the cabinet, there's a big wooden bowl. He lifts it down.

"My, my," he says. "What have we here?" He hands the bowl to me.

It's Beatrice! She sits in the bowl, blinking as if she just woke up. She probably did. "Big fat bird," she clucks to herself. She won't get out of the bowl until Richard pokes his finger at her. She climbs on and rides all the way to her cage, where he shuts the door.

But the thing is, he doesn't scold me, and neither does Dad.

"Birds do need to fly," says Richard, who decides to let her out more.

After that weekend, Beatrice Strawberry gets to roam the house, even when I'm not there. She has plenty of adventures. And the best thing is that she starts calling me at my mom's house. Well, usually Richard dials, or sometimes my dad, but then they put Beatrice right on.

She's not a bad conversationalist, if you don't expect what she says to make people sense.

"How's the flying going?" I ask her. "Getting any better at it?"

"Happy bird," says Beatrice.

"How's the diet going?"

"Treats."

And so on.

When I visit Richard and my dad, they let me take her into the shower with me. Beatrice sits on my shoulder and sings in the bathtub rain.

Despite all the practice she's getting, Beatrice is still clumsy at flying. But she rocks at hiding. Dad told me that the other day he couldn't find her. She wasn't in her favorite bowl. She wasn't moping around by the long window. Richard couldn't find her either. Finally, they heard her cackling. She had wedged herself between two postcards on their bulletin board.

"Fat bird" is what Richard said she said, but Dad swears she said "flat bird."

The best thing is, when Dad and Richard go to Italy again next summer, I get to take Bird home to Mom's for two whole weeks. I'm already wondering what she'll think of Tofu, and what Tofu will think of her!

9

India McAllister's Worst Wednesday Ever

It started like any other day. Most worst days probably do. There were no poisonous snakes in my bed, there was no mold on my toast. There was peach juice for breakfast, and I love peach juice. It was almost summer vacation. I walked out the door to school with Tofu, like I always do. It used to be Tofu, Colby, and me walking to school since his house is on my way to Wolfgang Elementary. Not anymore.

There are some rules that are written down, like the Constitution of the United States, with its famous signers and their swirly signatures, and our recess rules . . .

But some rules remain unwritten, like the one that says that Colby and I can't walk to school together anymore. It's not that he moved. It's just that we're in fourth grade. It's a pretty dumb rule, and it's all because of people like the Rodent. Also people like Mikey Smith and Zach Horton, who are big and stupid and in sixth grade, and say things like "Where's your little girlfriend, Colby? Where's China?" They call me that, even though they *know* my name. I mostly ignore them, except under my breath I am muttering, "Where's your brain, idiot?" That wouldn't be safe to say out loud to those guys!

But they don't get it. Colby is not my boyfriend. He's my *friend*. This is too hard to explain to people who don't listen anyway. It's easier to just not walk together. Colby usually takes his bike and plays football on the parking lot before school. He says he'd rather be walking with me, but it's complicated. So I walk to school with Tofu the Incredibly Intelligent, as in more than some people I know.

As Mom says, "That dog truly has street smarts."

He does!

I'm glad he comes with me. He's a good listener.

"Tofu," I say, "remember the old days when Colby walked with us?" Tofu looks at me and woofs. He likes Colby. Then he goes back to chasing squirrels. When Tofu goes somewhere, he's all about the side trips.

I do sometimes wish I walked with a person. But even though Amanda's house is on the next street over from mine, I'd rather die than walk with her. In fact I'd rather do a lot of things than walk to school with Amanda Roden.

Things I'd rather do than walk with the Rodent:

1. Eat dirt ... at least a little, clean dirt (organic).

   ←specks of dirt from my dad's garden

2. Hang out with Colby's sisters for a day, and they are a lot of work.

   Celia is 8 but thinks she's 14.

   Darby is 5, so that explains it!

   Monica is cute, but she wears diapers.

3. You name it!

So I walk with Tofu and pretend I don't care. This mostly involves keeping my chin way up and looking around like I have important things to see—things that are much better noticed when you don't have anyone to talk with. Sometimes there *are* interesting things to notice, but mostly not.

By the time I get to Wolfgang Elementary, it's okay, because school is about to start and, mostly, I love school. I pat Tofu on the head and send him home. He usually goes directly home, says Mom, although he's taken some interesting detours over the years, including one involving skunks.

Everyone's out on the playground. Mikey is chasing people around with lip gloss he grabbed.

"Give it back!" yells Becca.

"Ew, lip gloss," yell all the boys.

I do not join in. Colby says hi by raising his eyebrow at me from across the parking lot, then the bell rings and he and I and everybody else walk into Mr. Argentoth's room. It's also the Rodent's room. We have only one class for each grade in Wolfgang because we're a really small town. That's fine with me, because, unlike *some* people, I'm not here to socialize. I'm here to learn!

I can't help it if I'm smart. I like reading. I like thinking. So what if some people think that's dumb? The joke's on them! And I love Mr. Argentoth. Not like lovey-dovey love. He's the furthest thing from handsome that there is. But he's just cool.

#1 STUDENT

It's like each of us is Mr. Argentoth's favorite, in our own way, because he understands EVERYbody!

Some examples:

Mitch almost never talks, but when he does, he's smart.

He knows that Nick always (always) has to doodle...

Lewis can usually find salamanders in the spring.

I, India, ♡♡♡ READING!

Amy has a special relationship with Alice, our fish.

Colby likes science, especially SPACE.

Believe it or not, he even likes the Rodent and lets her run practically all our errands to the office, which is very charitable of him

—or maybe he needs a break from her, too?

Today we start the day by talking about what to do with all the money we raised this year selling wrapping paper and magazines. Some of it is for our class trip to Boston. We're going to walk the Freedom Trail and go to a museum. We might even get to take the subway. I hope so. There's not a single subway in the whole state of Maine! But there's going to be leftover money, maybe because my neighbor, Mrs. O, bought five magazine subscriptions. She loves to read and sometimes she doesn't feel well enough to make it all the way to the library.

We say our ideas and Mr. Argentoth writes them on the board. Some of the ideas are good

and some of them are just plain selfish, and a few are good even if they are selfish.

We're all laughing and talking about our options when I notice something. Amanda is passing a note. There's nothing all that unusual about it except that she's passing it to Colby!

Colby unfolds the paper very slowly, under his desk. I can see, since my desk is now at the back of the room, probably because Mr. Argentoth can count on me to pay attention no matter what. I'm definitely paying attention to this. I watch Colby read the note. His mouth moves the way it does when he reads silently, like he's reading silently aloud. Then he blushes. I watch the red creep up his neck all the way to his ears. They are so bright red that I feel like rushing over with a fire extinguisher.

Then, while the rest of us keep talking about endangered species and possible pizza parties, I watch Colby tear a piece of paper from his blue binder. It's his math binder. I know, because sometimes he comes over to my house to do homework. He chews his pencil. He's thinking great big embarrassing thoughts. His ears are still on fire, along with the rest of him. He folds up the note and passes it to Joey, who passes it to Melanie, who passes it to the Rodent. She reads it, then she turns right around to look at him. Not only that, she's hugging the note to her chest and simpering.

I stare at my desk so hard that it practically cringes. I do not want to see this. Why would they be writing to each other? I try to think of some normal reasons.

REASONS

with footnotes
(like in research papers)

- Amanda is going to babysit Colby's little sisters?[1]

- Amanda asked Colby a math problem?[2]

13) 164,302

- Amanda is trying to make some other guy jealous?[3]

1. No. She's not old enough, or nice enough.
2. Why would she ask him?
3. Maybe . . .

Then I give up fooling myself and sit straight in my chair. I will just ignore this little problem.

It seems to work. The rest of the day is normal. Colby sits at my table at lunch. I'm at the girl end, and he's at the guy end. Amanda does not sit with us, since Riley does and Amanda thinks Riley smells. (He does, but at least he's nice.) Still, the whole day I'm full of suspicion that something else will happen.

It does.

After school, Amanda goes straight up to Colby. I watch as they leave, alone. Together. Talking. I almost barge right in, but it's like there's an invisible force field around them.

Melanie comes over to me and flings her hair around.

"I think he might like her, right?"

I don't know what to say to that so I just try to bravely smile, but it's possible that my face looks like I ate rat poison.

To top it all off, when I get home, Mom's not there and neither is Tofu. There's a note saying not to worry and that she took him to the vet to have a thorn taken out of his paw.

Poor Tofu! My baby is in pain!

Poor me! My best friend is a nincompoop.

This is my worst Wednesday ever.

10

The War of the Slippers and the Socks

After my worst Wednesday at school, things get a little better. It's not only because it's almost the weekend and soon I won't have to look at the Rodent making fluttery moon eyes at Colby and him blushing his head off. It's because Dad has to go to a medical conference in Cleveland and Richard is going, too. They wonder if Beatrice might be able to stay with *me*. It's not as far away as Italy, but they'll be gone for five days, and it sure beats waiting until next summer for her to meet Tofu!

"We could have one of the neighbors pop in to feed her," says Dad on the phone, "but we think she'll be too lonely."

"She might even pick at her feathers," says Richard, who is on the extension. He sounds worried. He doesn't need to convince me. I love Beatrice, too, bad habits and all.

"Yes!" I yell, without even checking with Mom. Then I talk to Beatrice on the phone for a while. I know Richard is holding the phone up to her beak, and that's very nice of him.

"Sweet Bird," says Beatrice. She has a very good self-image. I hold the phone up to Tofu's ear. He cocks his ear but isn't very conversational. He's more interested in my slipper. Tofu thinks it's his mortal enemy and that he has to chew it to pieces.

"Give me that!" I say. "Bird would never eat my slippers, silly dog!"

Mom says it's fine for Bird to visit us, and so it's settled.

Friday can't come soon enough for me. I make it through Thursday by keeping my nose in my book, even at recess. I sit on the bench dedicated to Mrs. Stachowiak (a teacher who died before I was born). I trace all the letters of her name with my little finger. The stone is cold to sit on but my book is great. It's about warrior mice, the kind of rodents I can stand.

Friday is the day Beatrice Strawberry Bird is coming, so who cares if Amanda is still on her Colby campaign? Besides, I win the class spelling bee, like I always do, by spelling the word *hypocrite*. Amanda doesn't even know what that *means*.

"I think they're really in love," Melanie says hotly into my ear as we all leave for the weekend. "You know, Colby and Amanda?" It's exactly the kind of news she lives to tell . . . the sort of news that is happening right in front of your eyes and you'd have to be a moron not to notice.

I know she is waiting for me to respond, but I just shrug and keep stuffing books into my backpack. Out of the corner of my eye, I see my former best friend and the stupid giggling Rodent, but I choose not to think about it. Bird is coming, I tell myself, not even looking at Melanie. Who cares about Colby? But it does hurt because I'd been planning for him to meet Beatrice, and now, obviously, he can't. He's a traitor.

Beatrice is there when I get home.

"Your father and Richard had to catch a plane," says Mom. "Bird's in the dining room. I must say she's beautiful."

I agree, and so does Bird. She's singing her "Pretty Bird Pretty Bird" song. The sun streams in and the walls are blue. Being in our dining room is a bit like being outside, and I think Bird's gone happily hyper. No offense to Richard and Dad, but their condo is kind of dark. I'm so thrilled to have her here that I almost call Colby, but then I remember. I can't.

Fortunately, I'm very busy with Bird.

I'm so busy that I accidentally ignore Tofu. He doesn't like being ignored unless he's doing something really bad. Maybe that's why he's *eating* my best blue slipper, the one with the bunny ears (or, should I say, the one that *used* to have bunny ears) . . . so me ignoring him will work in his favor. He's not merely chewing . . . he's *swallowing*!

"No, Tofu," I yell at him. "Bad dog!" He skulks away under the dining room table, and I immediately feel rotten. He's just jealous. I know that feeling. "Come here, baby dog," I say in my cuddliest voice. "I love you so much." Tofu crawls out from under the table and puts his head in my lap. "You're my best boy," I tell him, and I'm glad that Bird is probably a girl.

Then I get this idea.

I'll close up the dining room and let Beatrice out. Why not? Where could she go? Maybe she'd like to say hello to Tofu, out from behind her bars. That is the problem with birds and little animals—you have to be their jailer. Besides, she's used to some freedom at Dad and Richard's.

"Okay," I say to Bird, offering her my finger. "Time to play." She hops right on and starts preening herself, but I can tell she's eyeing Tofu. He's eyeing her, too. I can almost feel their vision rays.

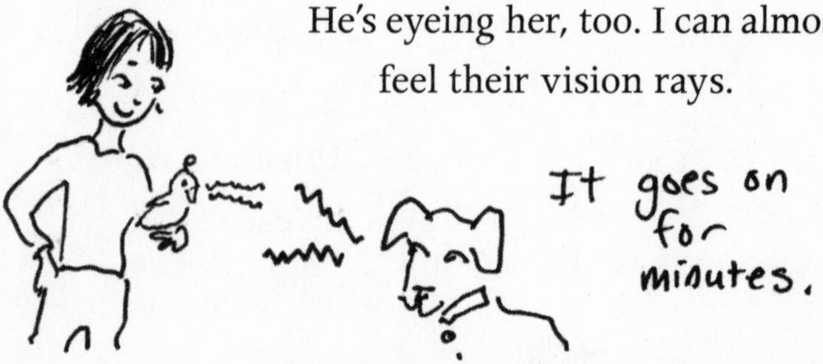

Then, all of a sudden, she makes her move. With full landing gear out, Bird swoops down onto Tofu's back. He jolts in surprise and his eyes open wider than the first time he ate ice cream.

"It's okay, boy," I tell him. "That's your new friend, Bird."

Tofu makes the tiniest whimper and twists his head around. I'm surprised I'm not nervous. He could easily bite her. Then again, she could easily rise up into the air and escape or peck his nose to pieces with her beak of steel. But exactly what I hope will happen happens, and it is *so* cool. Within a minute, Beatrice is riding around on Tofu's back, just like I pictured it.

After a good long tour of the dining room, Tofu plops down and refuses to get up. Beatrice shrieks "strawberries!" for some reason and flies down under the table, where Tofu has left my poor bunny slipper. Oh, no, I think. That's Tofu's personal, private enemy. What will happen next? But Beatrice just gives my earless slipper a peck and then flies around the room. Since we don't really use our dining room to actually eat in (it's way too big for just us), there's a pile of laundry on the table, waiting to be folded. Bird dives into the basket and comes up with my polka-dot sock. She gives it a good shake and flings it to the floor.

Tofu pounces and growls at the sock and Beatrice Bird hops back up to my finger. Then Tofu goes wild-dog crazy and runs back under the table to get the slipper. Bird flies back down to the sock and cackles with glee. They're both totally vanquishing their foes. I'm glad somebody can, I guess.

"Come here, baby dog," says Bird, because she heard me say it *once* and she's that smart. Tofu looks up from his dead slipper, all confused.

"Okay, you guys," I say, "time out." Even though my slipper is wrecked and my sock is pecked, I want to feel like the victor. To the victor belong the spoils, plus they're mine anyway. I can smell Mom's lasagna cooking, and it's a special occasion when Mom cooks, that's for sure.

Tonight, we eat in the dining room, with the unfolded laundry right next to us, Tofu under the table, and delightful Bird back in her cage.

"What do you say to a little *La Traviata*?" Mom asks. She likes to play loud opera when we eat home-cooked meals, to make it even more special.

"Sure," I say, feeling generous since I get to have Bird here. Opera's not my favorite music. I think it's strictly for grown-ups.

It turns out that opera makes Bird twitchy, too. It's like she wants to sing along but hasn't quite gotten the words down. So she throws a hissy fit, but it's hilarious.

Mom and I spend the evening playing checkers, folding laundry, and watching Bird the Prima Donna and Tofu the Valiant Slipper Warrior. I hardly miss Colby at all.

11

India McAllister Is Officially an Idiot

On Sunday, the worst Wednesday ever begins to look like a picnic. That's because I end up having the biggest adventure of my life without being any kind of hero. The day starts bright and beautiful. Sunshine pours into the room. Bird is still visiting and acting adorable. She flies around the room, chasing the shadows of clouds. Then she swoops down to the dog. She and Tofu could be a circus act, they're that fun to watch. But watching by myself is *boring*. Mom's in her studio. She's painting what she calls an epic scene, so I know she won't stop to make lunch. I make the mistake of calling Colby. He's just the same old Colby, I tell myself. Maybe he's come to his senses. I dial his number. I get his little sister, Celia.

"Cece," I say, since that's her nickname, "could I talk to Colby?"

"Nope," says Cece.

"Okay," I say. "Why not?" If you don't ask her, she won't say a thing. Some people probably shouldn't be answering the phone.

"He's not here," says Cece.

Then I make my big mistake. "Where is he?" I ask.

"Out with Amanda," says Cece, and hangs up on me.

My stomach gets totally sour. I sit down at the kitchen table. Tears begin to pour down my face. I make sure Bird is safely in her cage. I pat Tofu on the head. I have to go somewhere to be alone.

I head toward the woods behind our house. I hop over the stone wall, without even wondering if I'll see the garter snake who lives there. I pretend not to see Mrs. O, who is waving at me from her window.

My feet and Mom's have worn a narrow path into the forest. Mostly my feet. When I was younger, I'd come into the woods to think about my birth mom. I'd come without Tofu, since he'd cheer me up too much and I actually *wanted* to be sad. Besides, he scares away the wildlife. I always wrote "Dear Birth Mother" notes and hid them under rocks. I did that because my old idea of sending balloons with notes tied to the strings wouldn't really work. They would burst way before they crossed the Pacific Ocean and a bird might mistake the dead balloon for food and choke. How could a birthday party balloon make it all the way to China from Maine? It wouldn't even make it from Wolfgang to China, Maine, and there *is* one. Besides, my birth mom probably doesn't read English.

Sometimes I look for my old notes, but they're mostly decomposed.

Dear Chinese Mother.
I wish I could remember you!
♡ India (Fei)
Nature takes my notes and rains on them so they compost into the earth and that's fine with me because really these are notes for nobody (but me).
Why? Why? Why?
crumple
crumple
crumple

It's funny how you can think really hard about a person you don't know. It's also funny how, when you try not to think about something, then that's all you can think about. Colby and Amanda, Colby and Amanda, Colby and Amanda. How can Colby *like* the *Rodent*?

I walk furiously into the woods, not really noticing how springy it's getting. The little creek rushes with water. Blackflies cloud the air. Let them bite me. I'm too sad to care. Bloody bites would fit my mood just fine.

By the time I stop to rest, I'm someplace in the woods I don't recognize. There's an old snowmobile rusting next to some swamp irises. There's a little pond, with water bugs skittering all over it. I can't hear Route 16 at all, maybe because there's no traffic on it, or maybe because it's too far. There are a *lot* of trees.

I don't think I've ever been this far in the forest before.

I sit on the soft moss to think, which is not good for the moss. It dies if you bother it. But today I am not thinking of botany. I curl up into a little itchy ball of blackfly bites and fume.

Before I know it, I'm waking up from a weird dream. In my dream I was in China. It was very green with hills, and the wind was blowing something awful. I was freezing. When I open my eyes I can see why. Big, fat, wet snow is falling—even though it's June! This happens sometimes but not much. "Poor man's fertilizer," my dad calls it. "Good for the gardens." I'm not sure why. Minerals, maybe? It's freaky to have snow in almost summer!

Snowflakes dance down. They are white and beautiful against the green fir trees. Looking up, I almost feel like I'm flying myself, and the cold, cold flakes numb the tears and the blackfly feeling off my face. But it's cold and I'm not wearing my jacket. I don't have my boots. This is crazy. I have to go home.

But there's a problem—I'm actually lost. I wish I had Tofu with me. Tofu is never lost.

The trees all look the same, especially with

the snow that's sticking to them. My little deer path is covered up with white. I was so angry

when I headed into the woods that I forgot to notice landmarks. Maybe I'm not even in Wolfgang anymore. I could be clear over to Chesterville. It's hard to tell which direction I'm going in, since there's no more sun. Just snow that's falling, falling, falling!

India McAllister is officially an idiot. And maybe done for. I've heard of people getting lost for days without their coats. This sometimes doesn't turn out well.

"Help me!" I yell between sniffles. "I'm lost in here!" But nobody answers.

I know you're supposed to stay put in the woods, to make a little shelter. But I start running in the direction I think must be right. The snow makes it slippery. I fall over a log and gash my arm, but it hardly hurts since I'm frozen solid like an ice-cream bar. By the time I get to a deep ravine, I stop. I can't go farther. It's all wrong and also very dark, despite the snow.

I curl up under a hemlock to think. I hope somebody finds me. A nice somebody, like Colby's dad out hunting even though it's not hunting-for-anything season right now (except for turkeys). Or maybe a troop of Scouts could come by on a camping trip, all prepared with matches and blankets and granola bars.

I wouldn't even mind if
the Rodent found me,
as long as she didn't
talk to me and
knew the way out.
(But why would she?)

Hey—
There she is!
(Am I
famous
now?)

A little
ball
of
me

I decide I have to stay put. Walking around in circles is no good. Somebody will find me. I sing songs to myself and think of Tofu and Beatrice. But nobody comes, except the night. After a while it isn't snowing anymore. My clothes are damp. Even under these thick green branches, water dribbles down my neck. I hug the tree trunk as if it's my only friend in the whole world. Tears run down my cheeks. They are the warmest thing about this night. But I can't be lost *forever*! I start thinking terrible thoughts.

We miss her *so* much!

India? She was a good person.

I can't believe she's gone.

Mrs. Ordinance will have to put my photo in her wallet of lost people, but I sure hope she doesn't use my school photo, because I closed my eyes.

Then I get myself together. India McAllister will not give up, even if she's lost in a forest wearing wet clothes! People have survived much worse. I sing "Pop Goes the Weasel" over and over again loudly, since it's one of Beatrice's favorites and since I'll be much easier to find if I am noisy. Then I run out of breath.

An owl calls nearby. There is heavy crunching. I want to call out, but what if it's a big animal, like a wolf? I haven't heard any howling, thank goodness. The crunching comes closer. I crawl out from under the tree and look. There are voices and a light. It's the beam of a flashlight. It could be terrible robbers or something, but I decide to take that chance.

"Hello," I call. "Over here!"

"India?" shouts an unfamiliar voice. "India!"

I answer, and the person strides into view. It's two people, actually, some kind of warden and my mother. And not only that, it's Tofu! Tofu on a leash, straining to reach me. Tofu, my hero dog who trailed me through the cold, dark woods so I could be found!

"Mom," I sob. "Tofu. I love you so much." Mom hugs me hard and wraps me in my big winter coat. Tofu licks all the tears off my face.

"Oh, honey," Mom says. "Thank goodness Mrs. O saw you go into the woods. And the snow, oh, the snow. We were so worried!" It seems like she wants to say a whole lot more, but she just holds me tight and rocks me back and forth until I'm nearly warm.

It's like a sappy scene in a movie, but one that feels good . . .

It takes us over an hour to come out of the woods. The warden and Tofu keep us going in the right direction. The warden doesn't say much and I'm glad about that because I do feel foolish, now that I'm found.

"Quite the storm," he does say, although it isn't snowing anymore.

"Yup," I agree.

Mrs. O comes over the minute we get home. She's been waiting up for us with cranberry oatmeal cookies, straight from the oven. "I just knew you'd be found," she says, smothering me in a hug. Then Dad calls from Cleveland, since I guess Mom let him know I was missing.

"India," he says, "my strong girl. I'm so relieved! I'll be home in two days, and I can't wait to see you!" He says he can't believe there was a snowstorm, but then again he can. This is Maine, after all. We talk a little bit about how Beatrice is liking Tofu and everything, then we say good night. "Richard sends you a big hug," Dad says before he hangs up. I've never hugged Richard in person, at least not yet, but I think someday I will.

I fall asleep in my own bed after checking in on Beatrice Strawberry Bird. She's singing as if nobody in the world has any problems whatsoever. It's very sweet, but I cover her cage with a towel. It's already eleven o'clock. To me, it feels like next Thursday. Mom still calls some other people, to let them know I've been found. (Fortunately, none of them is Amanda the Rodent.) Mom washes my arm gash and covers my wound in a mermaid Band-Aid, the kind I liked when I was six. My arm throbs, just a little.

"Sweetie," Mom says when I explain how sad and mad I was. "I'm sure Colby is still your friend." She reassures me that the Rodent never has to find out that I got myself lost in the snowstorm. She tells me a story I've heard before, about how when she was little she had an enemy named Barbara, who grew up to be one of her best friends. "So you never know," she says wisely. Although I do know. The Rodent and I will never be friends.

Mom sits by my bed, holding my hand until I'm back in Dream China, walking those green hills all the way until morning.

In my dream, I am a long-ago girl who knows dragons and mist.

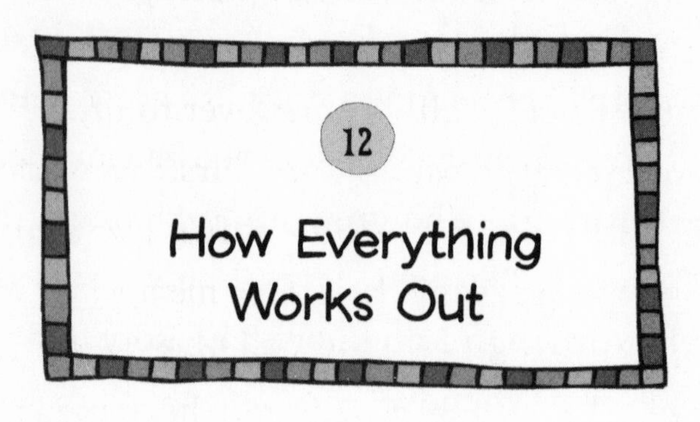

12

How Everything Works Out

Mom says I don't have to go to school on Monday, so I can recover from my accidental adventure. Even though Beatrice is visiting, I still want to go. It's like getting back on your horse. That's what brave people do. There aren't that many school days left. Anyway, after all that sad time in the woods, even seeing the Rodent doesn't seem that bad.

School is fine today. It's better than fine, actually. That's because Colby is not even *looking* at Amanda. Better yet, she's ignoring him completely.

After school, Colby comes over to my house without me even asking him. First, we admire Bird. Bird rides around on Tofu's back while singing the opera that she's now memorized and invites herself to Colby's shoulder. Her claws pinch him, but he stands still and takes it. I can tell they like each other.

The back hall stairs by the kitchen

Then, we play stairball. Stairball is this awesome game that you can play at my house because we have a wide stairway.

versus

one of Mom's paintings

The ancestors look very stern.

THE FRONT HALL STAIRS

We have a narrow and steep stairway, too, but those are the kitchen stairs and they're good for other things. Like hiding, because they're haunted and nobody dares search there.

My mom calls our front stairs the *Gone With the Wind* stairway. She doesn't mind if we play stairball. It's not like we lead movie- star lives with ball gowns or anything.

So Colby and I are hitting the ball back and forth up the stairs. You have to serve the ball with your fist, then step back so the other person can hit it. You get more points if you reach a higher stair, but if the ball stops on the landing, you have to go up there and beat it down. You do this by running, or by riding the banister. Tofu does the running part with you and only sort of gets in the way.

Stairball is a good time to talk about awkward stuff, because if you get misunderstood, you can always say, "That's not what I meant. You didn't hear me." The *thwack* of the ball and all the bouncing and laughing are good camouflage.

So I ask Colby about Amanda.

"Do you *really* like her?"

He hits the ball to the eleventh stair and shrugs. "She's in love with my brother Jacob."

I want to laugh at him—he looks so sad—and jump for joy because I'm so happy. But I restrain myself, like best friends do.

"Too bad for him," I say and grin.

Later, when we're having macaroni and cheese with peas in it, and listening to the awesome

Beatrice do her crazy best at opera, I tell Colby about my long time in the deep woods.

"In the snowstorm?" he asks. "Wow."

I nod. "I think I might have seen abominable snowman prints." Then I laugh, and he laughs, because both of us know I am just making that part up.

Colby smiles at me. "I'm glad Tofu found you."

At the sound of his name, Tofu presents his ears for scratching, and Colby knows exactly the spot Tofu likes. We sit there, and Mom comes in with hot chocolate.

"June is an odd time to serve hot chocolate," she admits, offering us marshmallows. "But since it snowed yesterday . . ."

We don't complain. My mom's hot chocolate is right up there on the list of things that both Colby and I like. Anyway, there are three more days of school, so summer vacation is yet to come. That's almost better than having it actually here.

Some things are better *before* you actually get them...

Like:

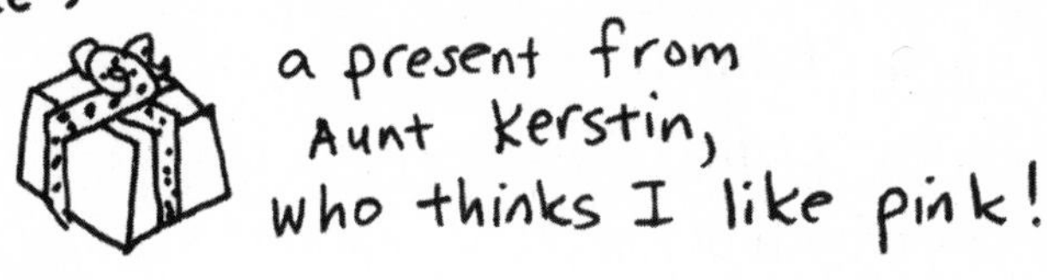

a present from Aunt Kerstin, who thinks I like pink!

a girly pink headband

very, very pink mittens

and pink pony notebooks (ick!)

...and some things are not:

ice cream from Harvey's (It's always *more* amazing, especially the pistachio!)

The next day, Dad is back from Cleveland. After school, Mom surprises me by saying that she's going to drive me and Beatrice over to Ottenbury. That's almost never happened before. Dad usually gets me himself. Ever since I lost myself in the woods, Mom's been acting like I might be a bit younger than I am. But that's okay.

"Let's take Tofu, too," she suggests, "since he and Beatrice get along so well. The whole family can go."

Tofu's always up for a ride. We put Beatrice's cage, with her in it, on the front seat, next to Mom, and buckle it in with the seatbelt. Tofu and I get in the back. Mom rolls the window down for Tofu, so he can stick his nose out and smell all the new summer smells. It's good, because then his slobber can go outside, not on me.

As we ride along the back roads to Ottenbury, Beatrice Strawberry Bird starts chirping and talking.

"Funny dog," she announces. "Bird loves Tofu, Tofu, Tofu."

Tofu pulls his head inside the car for a moment and looks around. Then he goes back to the business of detecting distant trash bins and other tantalizing things. He's so happy, he starts to howl out the window, and I'm sure we look very funny in Mom's messy old car. That's okay—there's nobody to see us.

When we get to The Pines and pull into Dad and Richard's driveway next to the three cars they can't fit into their garage, there *is* someone to see us. It's that nosy neighbor from next door. I feel a bit sorry for her, spying on us from behind her curtain. She should just come out and meet the gang.

Dad and Richard greet us. After Dad has scooped me into his arms and squeezed me wicked hard, he turns to Mom.

"Thanks so much for bringing her, Rosemary," he says, in a friendly way. Mom nods and smiles, as Tofu does his happy-dog leaps. He's been missing Dad, I think. Meanwhile, I'm hugging Richard. He smells like cologne and his arms are stiff, but that's just Richard. Maybe he needs more hugging practice.

"Thank you so much for taking care of Beatrice," Richard says to me.

"Our pleasure," Mom answers for all of us.

Before we leave, we all go out on Dad and Richard's back deck to have some tea. I use four lumps of sugar and nobody says anything. It's mostly because I can't resist their weird sugar tongs that look like chicken feet.

"Nice tomato plants," Mom tells Dad. "They're looking hardy."

"Thanks." Dad smiles, and he doesn't even fret when Tofu goes over to investigate the garden, his whole body wagging with delight. "Let's hope so."

"Before long, we'll have lovely tomatoes," Richard says. "Probably too many tomatoes. We can send some home to you with India, when she visits."

We all like that idea. Especially me.

Sometimes, sitting quietly
without talking
says more than words, like
when you're all together
and the summer
is about to begin!

The End